USBORNE

Usborne
A Sticker Dolly Story
Ice Palace

Zanna Davidson

Illustrated by Katie Wood

Cover illustration by Antonia Miller

Use the stickers to dress the Dolls on the 'Meet the Dolls' pages

Meet the Princess Dolls

Meera, Sophia and Olivia are the 'Princess Dolls'. They help the princesses who live on the Majestic Isle, with everything from new outfits to royal emergencies.

Meera

is brilliant at making clothes and jewellery. She is generous and giving, and also likes to follow royal rules.

Use the stickers to dress the Dolls

Olivia

is a rebel princess. She spends as much time as she can outside. She loves plants and animals and is an excellent horse rider.

Sophia

loves books and stories about princesses of the past. She is always calm in a crisis. Her favourite place in the world is the palace library.

Dolly Town

The Princess Dolls live in the Royal Palace, in Dolly Town, home to all the Dolls. The Dolls work in teams to help those in trouble and are the very best at what they do, whether that's fashion design, ice skating or puppy training. Each day brings with it an exciting new adventure...

The **Shooting Star** train whisks the Dolls away on their missions.

Madame Coco's **Costume Emporium** has everything the Dolls might need.

The Dolls love to celebrate at the **Cupcake Café.**

Animal Sanctuary

Rose Theatre

Bluebell Bookshop

Evergreen Sports Arena

Royal Palace is home to the Princess Dolls.

Palm Tree Film Studios

Heartbeat Dance Academy

Fashion Design Studio

Mission Control Centre lets the Dolls know who's in trouble and where to go.

Pop Star Stadium

Silver Sparkles Skating Rink

Strawberry Lane Stables

Honeysuckle Cottage

Chapter One
The Missing Tiara

Meera and Sophia sat by the hearth in the Royal Palace, warming their hands over the dancing flames. Even though it was only early afternoon, the light was already beginning to fade.

"Winter is definitely coming," said Meera. "I hope we'll have snow soon."

"Oh, me too!" said Sophia. "I've already started thinking about our midwinter celebration. Shall we have a ball like last year?"

"Or we could do something different," said Meera. "I'm writing a list of everyone we should invite."

The Magic Dolls

The Ballet Dolls

The Animal Rescue Dolls

The Pop Star Dolls

As she spoke, the door opened and Olivia stepped inside. "I've been checking on the horses," she explained, taking off her hat and coat. "I wanted to make sure they were warm enough in their stables. It's so cold outside, the palace lake has nearly frozen over."

"Come and sit by the fire," said Sophia. "We were just talking about the midwinter celebration," she went on. "What do you think our party should be this year?"

Olivia looked thoughtful, but before she could answer, the Dolls' watches started flashing.

Meera hurried over to the table and picked up her gold-cased screen. She tapped on the flashing tiara symbol.

"Mission Control here!" came a voice. "Are the Princess Dolls there?"

It's the Snow
Princess on
the Majestic Isle.
Her baby sister's Naming
Ceremony is today, and she's
meant to be wearing the Ice
Diamond tiara...but she's lost it.

Meera gasped and turned to
the others.

"The Ice Diamond Tiara is
famous – there's nothing else like
it. It's made up of hundreds of tiny

shining diamonds and its centre is a beautiful blue diamond.

It's been passed down from Snow Princess to Snow Princess for generations. It's even rumoured to have magical properties..."

"I've heard of it too," said Sophia. She ran down the corridor to the palace library and came back with a huge, leather-bound tome, its pages edged with gold.

"This book is all about the jewels of the Majestic Isle," Sophia explained. "Here's the page on the Ice Diamond Tiara."

THE ICE DIAMOND TIARA

The Ice Diamond tiara has, at its centre, a large flawless brilliant-cut blue diamond.

"This tiara sounds very precious indeed," said Sophia.

"The poor Snow Princess," added Olivia. "She must be so worried. We have to help her find it."

"I agree," said Meera. She tapped her screen. "Of course we'll help," she told Mission Control.

"Mission details coming through now," replied Mission Control.

Search for the
Ice Diamond Tiara

Mission details:

Find the Ice Diamond Tiara before the Naming Ceremony at 6pm.

The Naming Ceremony is to take place at the Ice Palace, in the Snow Kingdom on the Majestic Isle.

Crystal, the Snow Princess, will be waiting for you on the Frozen River.

CRYSTAL THE SNOW PRINCESS

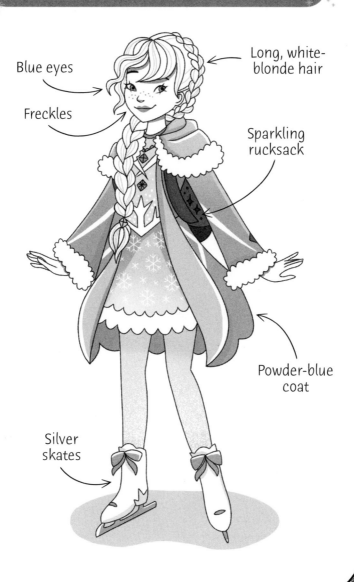

Blue eyes

Freckles

Long, white-blonde hair

Sparkling rucksack

Powder-blue coat

Silver skates

MISSION LOCATION:

Snow Kingdom

Ice Palace

Frozen Lake

Border of
River Kingdom

"I've always longed to go to the Ice Palace," said Meera. "It's made entirely from ice, with glittering turrets, and palace gardens full of ice sculptures."

"But look," said Olivia, pointing at the map. "The Snow Princess is miles upriver. She's a long way from the Ice Palace. I wonder what she's doing there?"

"And we haven't got long until the Naming Ceremony," said Sophia, checking her watch. "It's three o'clock already."

"We'll have to hurry," said Meera.

The Princess Dolls put on their coats and dashed down the grand palace steps.

"And now," said Sophia, "we just need some *really* warm clothes. It's time to visit…"

"…Madame Coco's Costume Emporium!" they chanted.

Chapter Two

A Trip to Madame Coco's

The Dolls huddled close as they walked to Madame Coco's, trying to brace themselves against the chill wind.

"At last!" said Sophia, as Madame Coco's came into view. The light spilled out from the store windows, casting a glow over the pavement.

The Princess Dolls hurried into the welcoming warmth, and quickly made their way to the famous glass elevator.

"Hello, Princess Dolls," said Jasper, the lift attendant, raising his cap.

"Hello, Jasper," said Meera. "Can you take us to the Royal Department Floor, please."

We're on an urgent mission.

Jasper pressed the button for floor number six and the next moment, the glass elevator was whooshing up and up before coming to a stop with a gentle

TING!

The Dolls stepped out into a large room, lined with a plush red carpet and full of shining jewels and glittering dresses.

"Ah! Princess Dolls," came a voice, and Madame Coco glided around the corner.

"I wasn't expecting you. Have you received a new mission?"

"We have," said Sophia. "The Snow Princess has lost the Ice Diamond Tiara and we have to help her find it!"

"If you're off to the Snow Kingdom, then I had better find you some warm clothes," said Madame Coco. "Now let me see. You'll need thick, fleecy boots, padded coats…"

She made her way around the room, picking out items, followed by a line of assistants.

Meera's clothes

Embroidered emerald-green coat, with gold-trimmed sleeves

Dark gold belt

Fleecy boots

Olivia's clothes

Quilted, fleecy-white jacket

Pale blue, thick fleecy trousers

Silky-soft earmuffs

White, lace-up snow boots

Sophia's clothes

Embroidered
purple jacket with
fleece-lined hood

Star
hair clip

Soft snow
boots

Long purple
star-studded skirt

"Thank you, Madame Coco!"
said Olivia. "These look fantastic."

"And warm!" added Sophia,
gratefully.

"Now try them on," smiled
Madame Coco, ushering the
Dolls towards the changing
rooms.

Their names flashed above
the changing room doors. The
Princess Dolls stepped inside and
when they stepped out again…

"Now you're *almost* ready for the Snow Kingdom," said Madame Coco. "Just two more things to give you…" As she spoke, she handed them each a pair of ice skates.

"Everyone in the Snow Kingdom travels around by skating on the Frozen River," she explained. "And last but not least, these are for you," she added, giving each of them an elegant silver case.

The Dolls peeked inside, to see they each had a glittering pair of shoes, and a tiara.

"After all," said Madame Coco,
"a princess should never be without
a tiara! Now, you'd better be going…"

"Thank you!" said Sophia, and
with a wave, the Dolls hurried back
outside, onto the lamplit street.

Meera tapped the tiara symbol
on her watch. A moment later,
the Shooting Star train appeared

in a glittering cloud.

"Hello, Princess Dolls," said
Sienna, the train driver. "Where
can I take you today?"

"The banks of the Frozen River
please," said Olivia, "on the
Majestic Isle." She held up the
mission map for Sienna to see.

The doors of the Shooting
Star closed behind them,
and with a

WHOOSH

they were off, whizzing
through Dolly Town and into
a dark tunnel, sparkling with
hundreds of tiny stars.

When they shot out the other side, the Dolls gasped. "This must be the Snow Kingdom," said Sophia. "It's beautiful!"

All around them were snowy forests, the thick green trees looking as if they had been dusted with icing sugar.

The train came to a stop on the banks of the Frozen River, where the forest ended and tiny shoots of grass poked up through the powdery snow.

The Dolls stepped outside, their breath misting the air.

"Good luck, Princess Dolls!" called Sienna, as the Shooting Star pulled away. The Dolls looked around. Everything seemed silent and empty.

"I wonder what the Snow Princess was doing here," said Sophia. "And where she is now…"

Chapter Three

The Frozen River

The Princess Dolls waited on the bank, scanning the river for any sign of the Snow Princess. A light breeze ruffled the branches, causing flurries of snow to drift to the ground.

Then came a *swoosh*, and in a
blur of speed, the Snow Princess
skated around the bend on the
Frozen River.

Her silver skates flashed in the
low winter sun, while
her coat billowed
behind her in
the wind.

"Oh! Princess Dolls!" said the Snow Princess when she reached them. "I'm so glad you're here. I'm Crystal."

"We came as soon as we could," said Sophia. "But why are you so far from the palace? We haven't got long before the Naming Ceremony starts."

"I know!" said Crystal. "It's a

disaster. I don't know where to begin…"

"Tell us the whole story," said Olivia, gently.

"Okay," said Crystal, giving her a grateful smile. "It all started when I found out that the Skating Championships were on the same day as my sister's Naming Ceremony.

You see, I *really* wanted to go to the championships. I love ice skating and I'd practised and practised my piece – I even thought I might win.

But when I asked my parents they said I couldn't go in case I was late for the ceremony."

"So what happened?" Olivia asked.

"I was sure I'd have time to do

both," said Crystal. "So, this morning, I packed everything I'd need for the Naming Ceremony, including the Ice Diamond Tiara, and I crept out of the palace to go to the championships. My plan was to skate there and back along the Frozen River.

But I hadn't even reached the championships before I realized my parents were right – I'd never make it in time. So, I decided to turn back and that's when I saw my bag had split open…and the Ice Diamond Tiara was missing!"

She showed the Dolls her bag as she spoke. Inside was a gorgeous blue gown and a sparkling diamond necklace, but no tiara.

"It must have fallen out," said Crystal. "But I've been up and down this stretch and I can't find it anywhere."

"Do you know where it might have fallen out?" asked Meera.

"I'm sure it was somewhere around here," said Crystal. "I remember my bag catching on one of those low-hanging branches, but there's no sign of the tiara now

and I can't go to the ceremony without it. Everyone will be expecting me to wear it – it's a famous heirloom! But if I don't turn up to the Naming Ceremony I'll be in even *more* trouble. I don't know what to do!"

"Don't worry," said Meera. "We're here to help now. First things first – let's split up to search the area. Olivia and Crystal, why don't you search the river up until that curve? Sophia, could you check downriver? And I'll scour the banks."

"We'll have to be careful," said
Olivia, pointing to the clouds
above the forest.

"There's a thick fog coming in.
Let's not go too far away from
each other. We'll use our mission
watches to keep in touch."

"Oh dear," said Sophia. "That fog is going to make the tiara even harder to find. Let's work as quickly as we can."

The Dolls pulled on their skates and set off along the river.

While Olivia, Sophia and Crystal searched the icy surface, Meera kept her eyes fixed on the snowy banks.

She was hoping to see the glinting light of the Ice Diamond, but there was nothing but snow, and the fog was growing thicker and thicker. Soon, she could barely see her own hands.

Meera was about to call out to the others, when she noticed some marks in the snow.

Peering closer, she realized they were a trail of paw prints. Each was about the size of her hand, topped by five claw marks.

Bear tracks!

She pressed the tiara symbol on her mission watch to summon the others and turned on its torch to shine through the fog.

A few minutes later, the others came skating through the mist.

"Have you found the tiara?" asked Crystal.

"I'm afraid not," Meera replied. "But I have found these," she added, pointing to the paw prints. "I think they're bear tracks."

Olivia bent down for a closer look. "They are," she agreed. "But from the size of them, I think it's just a cub."

"I'm sure this is where my bag snagged on a branch," said Crystal, pointing to a low-hanging tree just beside her. "Look! Here are some of the threads from my bag, caught on these twigs."

"Maybe the bear cub went off with your tiara?" said Sophia. "The cub could have been playing with it."

"There's just one problem," said Olivia. "Where there's a bear cub, the mother bear is never far away. Do we dare go after them?"

Chapter Four
Tracks
in the Snow

The Princess Dolls stared at the bear tracks, deep in thought. Then they looked up and exchanged glances. They all knew what the other was thinking.

"We don't have a choice, do we?" said Olivia.

Sophia shook her head.

"We have to follow the tracks," said Meera. "It's our only lead."

"Thank you," said Crystal, her voice full of relief.

"We're going to have to move fast," added Olivia. "We don't have much time."

"I've got an idea," said Sophia, suddenly, her eyes lighting up. "Shall I see if I can find another way to get us to the palace? If we do find that tiara, we want to be sure Crystal's back in time for the Naming Ceremony."

"Good thinking," said Meera. "We'll let you know if we're in luck."

The others waved goodbye to Sophia. Then they quickly

took off their ice skates and put
on their snow boots. With their
skates slung over their shoulders,
they set off up the snowy
bank, following the
bear tracks.

"The tracks are taking us away from the river..." Crystal pointed out.

"...and up a *very* steep hill," added Meera, slightly breathlessly.

They wound their way through the snow-covered trees, eyes to the ground. The snow was starting to fall again, and they didn't want to lose sight of the tracks. The forest hillside seemed muffled in silence by the falling snow.

"We're losing valuable time," Meera whispered to Olivia. "I really hope this does lead us to the tiara."

"I know," Olivia whispered back. "But it can't be long now. A bear cub this size wouldn't stray too far from its mother."

"Oh look!" Crystal called suddenly. "Up ahead. I think the tracks are leading us to that cave in the hillside."

"You're right," said Olivia, following the line of bear tracks in the dim light. "Let's approach as softly as we can."

They carried on quietly, the only sound the crunch of the snow underfoot. When they reached the cave, Olivia gestured for Crystal to stand behind them. Then Meera and Olivia peered around the entrance of the cave.

Meera gave a little gasp. The cave was dark within but lit by a strange blue light that cast flickering shadows across the glittering snow.

Together, Meera and Olivia
peered deeper inside.

"There, at the back!" said Olivia,
pointing. "Can you see it? I'm
sure it's a bear cub."

"It's so dark,

I can't make it out," said Meera.
"We'll have to use our torches."

She swiped the screen on her
watch, so the cave was lit by a
beam of light. And there, at the
back, was a tiny bear cub.

"Oh!" gasped Olivia. "Isn't it adorable."

"And what's more," added Meera, "just look what's in its mouth. It's the Ice Diamond Tiara! I can't believe it!"

Unable to resist, Crystal rushed into the cave to see.

"Oh my goodness!" she said. "We've found it at last."

"The cub must have found the tiara by the riverbank and brought it here," said Olivia. "Now, the tricky part is going to be persuading the cub to give it back to us!" She reached into her bag as she spoke. "Luckily," she said with a grin, "I have some snacks here which I think this bear cub will love."

She opened a small tub and

picked out some berries, then crouched down and held them out to the cub in the palm of her hand, talking gently all the time.

"Here you go, little cub," she said, her voice coaxing. "Come and try these."

The bear looked at her with his inky black eyes. For a moment he seemed to hesitate, then he padded forward, the tiara still gripped in his teeth.

He sniffed Olivia's hand, his black nose twitching in the torchlight.

Everyone held their breath, and then, trustingly, he dropped the tiara and began to lick up the berries.

Olivia had to try hard not to laugh as his warm tongue tickled her hand.

Slowly, so as not to alarm the cub, Meera reached forward to take the tiara.

"Is it okay?" whispered Crystal. "The bear cub hasn't broken it or chewed it, has he?"

"I think it's fine," Meera whispered

back, turning it over in her hand.
"Now, it's time for us to leave,
before the mother returns."

"She won't be happy if she finds
us with her cub," added Olivia.
"Mother bears are very protective
of their young."

They backed out of the
cave, Crystal first, but as
she looked down the
slope, she stopped in
her tracks.

"Oh no," she said.

"We're too late. There's a big bear between those trees…and she's coming straight for us!"

Chapter Five

Mamma Bear

The Princess Dolls watched the bear lumbering towards them. She was growling and her teeth were bared.

"She thinks we're a threat to her cub," said Olivia.

Her heart was beating fast but she was determined to keep the panic from her voice. "We'll never outrun her. We'll have to try walking away slowly."

"I'm not sure that's going to work," said Crystal. "Her eyes are fixed right on us."

"The Ice Diamond!" said Meera, staring down at the shining blue jewel. "That's what we need."

"What do you mean?" asked Olivia. "How is a diamond going to help us against a bear?"

"Do you know the legend?" asked Meera. "I've read that the tiara's light has the power to calm all creatures."

"I thought that
was just an old
story?" said Crystal.

"Well," said Meera,
taking a step forward.
"Now is the time to find out."

The bear was nearly upon them
now. She rose up on her back legs,
looming over them.

Meera held the Ice Diamond Tiara high above her head.

The mother bear stopped in her tracks, her gaze caught by its shining blue light.

Meera swung the tiara in her hands, and the bear followed her movements as if mesmerized, swaying slightly from side to side.

Oh! I think it's working!

"So do I!" breathed Crystal.

The bear slowly dropped down onto four paws. She stopped snarling and her dark eyes lost their ferocious stare. And then, a moment later, the bear cub came bounding out of the cave, and nuzzled up to his mother.

The bear looked down at her cub, drawing him close with her big paws.

"I think we're safe now," said Meera. "The bear's focused on her cub. It's almost as if she can't see us."

"Let's go," said Olivia. "But no running. We don't want to startle her." As slowly and calmly as they could, Meera, Olivia and Crystal backed away from the cave and headed down the hill, being careful to make as little noise as possible.

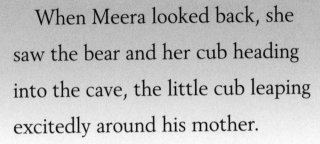

When Meera looked back, she
saw the bear and her cub heading
into the cave, the little cub leaping
excitedly around his mother.

"We've done it!" said Olivia.
"We've really done it! I'll let
Sophia know."

"I can't believe it," said
Crystal, gazing down at the tiara.
"It does have magical powers!"

"Either that or the bear really
loves diamonds," laughed Meera.

They all smiled as they made
their way to the banks of
the Frozen River, but when
they reached its icy shores,
Olivia looked at her watch
in alarm.

"I hadn't realized how late

it is!" she said. "I hope
Sophia's plan has worked,
or we'll never make it back to
the palace in time for the
Naming Ceremony."

But as she spoke, they heard
the sound of sleigh bells, and
there, racing through the forest,
came Sophia on a wooden
sleigh, pulled by a team of
reindeer. She drew up beside
them in a flurry of snow.

"Oh, Sophia!" said Olivia, reaching out to stroke a reindeer. "Wherever did you find that sleigh?"

"I followed our mission map to a farm," said Sophia. "I told them what had happened and the farmer

kindly lent me her sleigh."

"Now everyone," she went on, "jump aboard! If we ride like the wind, we should just make it to the palace in time!"

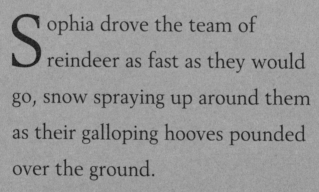

Chapter Six

Skating Under the Stars

S ophia drove the team of
reindeer as fast as they would
go, snow spraying up around them
as their galloping hooves pounded
over the ground.

"Just follow this path," said
Crystal. "It'll lead us straight to
the Ice Palace."

The sleigh path wound in and out of the Fir Tree Forest. They began to leave the Frozen River behind them, its frosty surface glittering silver and blue in the gathering dark.

At last, the Ice Palace came into view, icicle turrets rising above the trees of the forest.

"Wow!" gasped Meera. "It's even more beautiful than I imagined!"

I can't believe we're really here.

The reindeer came to a halt at the bottom of the palace steps. On one side, the Dolls could see a huge frozen lake, lit by glowing lanterns. On the other side, the palace seemed to shimmer in the dusky air.

"I'd better hurry inside and get changed," said Crystal. "But please," she added, "will you come to the Naming Ceremony? I'd really like you to be there."

"Thank you," said Meera.

"I'll see you in the Icicle Ballroom," said Crystal, as she jumped out of the sleigh. "Just follow the crowds!"

The Princess Dolls looked over
to see the other guests starting to
arrive. The air was filled with sleigh
bells as they saw guests dressed in
beautiful suits and gowns.

"Time to put on our tiaras and shoes," laughed Sophia. "Madame Coco really does think of everything."

One by one, the Princess Dolls opened up their cases and carefully slipped on their shoes and tiaras.

Then they hurried up the
palace steps and made their way
to the Icicle Ballroom.

The Princess Dolls gasped as
they entered. The room was lit by
flaming torches, the walls gleamed
an icy blue, and there were twin
thrones, carved from ice.

"Welcome everyone," said the King, stepping forward, "to our youngest daughter's Naming Ceremony."

As he spoke, an orchestra struck up, and the vast room was filled with music that echoed around the walls.

Everyone turned as the Queen entered, the tiny baby princess in her arms.

Behind them, carrying the baby's long white train, was Crystal, her head held high, the Ice Diamond Tiara shining its pure blue light.

When the Queen reached the centre of the room, she held up the baby princess for everyone to see.

"We would like to introduce you all to Princess Frostine!" announced the King and Queen together. And the Queen placed a tiny crown on the princess's head.

"Oh! Isn't she sweet?" said Olivia,

as the guests broke into applause.

"And look!" added Sophia.
"Over there! I can see the other
princesses from the Majestic Isle.
There's the River Princess…and the
Woodland Princess…Oh! And Cora,
the Cloud Princess."

After a speech from the King and Queen, the royal family proceeded through the crowds.

"Please join us in the Grand Dining Hall," announced the Queen, "where we'll be serving a feast to celebrate."

As soon as the Princess Dolls entered the Dining Hall, Crystal hurried over to them, followed by her parents.

The King and Queen held out their hands in greeting. "Crystal has told us what happened and how you helped her," said the Queen.

"I'm glad Crystal did the right thing in the end…" said the Queen. Then she turned to her daughter. "But we had no idea how much the Skating Championships meant to you. We're sorry you had to miss it."

"It was right that she did," said the King. "Her duty was to be with her family. But to make up for it…"

The King chimed the crystal glass in his hand, and called to the guests. "We have one more event for you tonight," he announced. "We'd like you all to join us by the Frozen Lake."

Then he turned to
Crystal. "How would you
like to perform your piece
now?" he said with a smile.

The Princess Dolls stood with
the other guests by the lake, its
frozen surface glittering beneath
the night sky, while Crystal twirled
across the lake on her skates. She
was as graceful as a
ballet dancer,

spinning, lifting and circling in the starlight.

"She really is talented, isn't she?" said Meera.

As Crystal's dance came to an end, the Princess Dolls clapped and cheered loudly.

Then, when the last of the guests had left, Crystal beckoned them over. "Would you like to skate too?" she asked. "I don't think there's anything more wonderful than skating beneath the stars."

"We'd love to," said Meera.

The Princess Dolls put on their
skates one last time and took to the
frozen lake. As she skated, Meera
drank in the stars, the beautiful ice

sculptures that gleamed in the
gardens and, most magical of all, the
Ice Palace itself, rising up behind
them, its turrets gleaming silver,
as if they were made of moonlight.

"What a wonderful end to the mission," said Sophia, as she finished her last lap of the lake.

Crystal hugged them goodbye. "Thank you," she said. "And please, do come and visit me again."

"We will," promised Meera.

Then Olivia pressed the tiara
symbol on her watch. "Mission
Control," she said, with a smile.

Mission complete.
Please send the
Shooting Star train.

Moments later, Sienna arrived
in a cloud of glittering dust.
"Where to, Princess Dolls?"
she asked.

"Back to Dolly Town and the

Cupcake Café, please," Meera
replied. "We want to celebrate."

"And warm up!" added Olivia,
laughing. "It's time for hot
chocolates all round!"

In the Cupcake Café, the Princess
Dolls took their favourite seats by
the window, smiling as Maya, the
Cupcake Café owner, brought
them all hot chocolates, piled high
with marshmallows.

"I loved going to the Majestic
Isle," said Meera. "And meeting
the Snow Princess."

"Me too," said Sophia. "And
now I know exactly how we
should help the Dolls of

Dolly Town celebrate midwinter…"

"Go on…" said Maya.

"Do tell!" added Olivia, stirring melted marshmallow into her chocolate.

"We can invite everyone to a frost fair around the palace lake!" said Sophia, grinning. "Picture the scene! It will be snowing by then and the trees will be glittering with frost. We can have music and food stalls and games…"

"Hooray!" cheered Olivia and

Meera. "That's a brilliant idea."

Then they placed their hands, one on top of each other. "Princess Dolls forever!" they chanted. "We can't wait for our next mission…"

The End

Join the **Princess Dolls** on their next adventure

PRINCESS DOLLS

A Sticker Dolly Story
Woodland Princess

Read on for a sneak peek…

Z ahra took a deep breath.
"It's all because of the
Royal Portrait," she began. "All my
brothers and sisters were so excited,
getting dressed up and putting on
their best clothes. My parents made
me put on this dress…but I made a
big fuss as I *hate* it. It's so long I can
hardly move in it without tripping
up, and then it's got these big puffy

shoulders and long sash so I can't
do anything…" She paused for a
moment, fiddling with the frayed
hem of her dress.

"Go on," said Olivia gently.

"Well, I did put on the dress
eventually, but my parents told me
not to go outside, so I wouldn't get
dirty. But I knew I'd never be able
to sit still for the portrait if I didn't

just have a quick run outside. But when I reached the glade, I realized I'd torn my dress on the spiky thorns and I knew my parents would be furious *and* think I'd done it on purpose, so that's when I asked for help. But as I waited for you to come, I just got angrier and angrier!"

"Why was that?" asked Olivia.

"I don't think I should even *be* in the Royal Portrait," said Zahra, miserably. "I don't like wearing dresses and jewels. All I really like doing is climbing trees, and my parents don't approve of that." She paused for a moment to wipe her face on her muddy sleeve. "I just don't think I make a very good princess…"

Edited by Lesley Sims and Stephanie King
Designed by Hannah Cobley and Jacqui Clark

First published in 2021 by Usborne Publishing Ltd.,
Usborne House, 83-85 Saffron Hill, London EC1N 8RT, England.
usborne.com Copyright © 2021 Usborne Publishing Ltd. UKE